# Every Sparrow Was
# Made to Fly

By Lin Thomas

Dear Alissandra,

Follow your dreams!

Lin Thomas

Copyright © 2018; All rights reserved;

YAY LEARNER LLC; Printed in the USA;

ISBN-13: 978-0-578-40537-7

# Every Sparrow Was Made To Fly

## By Lin Thomas

Illustrations by: Chitra Bhandare

*An inspirational story for kids ages 7-13 to achieve their dreams, develop confidence and accept challenges.*

YAY LEARNER LLC

*Dedication*

This book is dedicated to my father-in-law, Mattathilparampil Thomas (1926-2012), whom we lovingly referred to as Achayan. His grandchildren called him Apacha, an Indian word for Grandpa.

Achayan strongly believed that children must be happy and enthusiastic. He wished all his grandchildren to be "Chonakuttans" and "Chonakuttis" meaning "full of energy and zeal".

He encouraged everyone to eat healthy, live healthy, and make the most of life. He wanted to bring out the best in everyone. He remains alive in our memories, through his words of advice and the resonance of his laughter. May his positive spirit remain with all his grandchildren.

## Acknowledgements

*I would like to thank my parents Rajan and Lily for being constant sources of inspiration for me. I appreciate their unconditional love, and the spirit they have instilled in me. I thank my husband Jose, for encouraging me, and being my constant friend, counselor, critic and guide. I thank my children Melissa, Savia and Daniel for teaching me something new every day.*

*I am grateful to my sister Rini and my brother-in-law Bonny, for their feedback on my writing over the years. I thank Amma, my mother-in-law for teaching me to start my super busy day by entrusting everything to God, when I wake up in the morning. I am grateful to Omana aunty and all my dear friends for their support. Special thanks to Geena, Parvati, Mary (Suma) and Hanna for their support with this book. I thank our illustrator, Ms. Chitra Bhandare for bringing the story alive with her exceptional talent.*

*I would like to specially acknowledge all the children in my life, my 19 young nieces and nephews, my cousins, and all the children I have coached, for keeping the child in me always alive. I hope you all love this book*

*~ Lin Thomas*

# Contents

# 1

# The Beloved Mansion

"Sammy! Sammy!" I hear someone calling out, as I slip from the edge of a cliff. I try to grasp a branch but it slips through my fingers. I try to grasp at anything I can. Rocks, twigs... but I keep falling down the vast valley. "Help, Help!" I call out. My lips are moving but my voice can't be heard. It seems like someone pressed the mute button on the scene. I kick my legs but I keep falling and falling. The dark gray sky looks dreary. The rocks at the bottom look scary. There is no hope as I continue to fall. I see little birds fly away in a distance and close my eyes in despair.

Tring! Tring! I wake up startled. My hands are moist from sweating and I slam my alarm clock. What a horrible dream it was, not to mention it's the third time I have had this dream this month. What did it mean? Where was I falling?

I sigh and look at my familiar room with a sense of relief. My frown turns into a smile. It is summer break, and I have no school. Today my brother Zach and I are going to Georgy Uncle's mansion for a week-long vacation.

My name is Samelda Matthew, but everyone calls me Sammy. I am twelve and my brother Zach is fourteen. We live in Goa, a little state in India.

Georgy Uncle is my Papa's younger brother. Uncle's mansion is on the sandy shores of Bambolim, one of the popular beaches in Goa. The mansion is not too far away from our home, but it's my favorite vacation spot in whole wide world. Zach and I pack up our bags to leave.

2

"I'm going to miss you my little girl," Papa says to me as he drives us to Bambolim.

"Keep your sister out of trouble," he tells Zach with a wink.

Zach and I arrive at Bambolim. I run over to give a warm hug to Georgy Uncle.

The mansion had belonged to Apacha, my Grandpa. Georgy Uncle inherited it after Apacha's death. Pirates had lurked around the island, three hundred years ago. It was the perfect place to solve a mystery. I loved spending time at the old mansion and the little museum with pirate artifacts.

I have yearned for a mystery bottle that would come floating on the waves, encasing a treasure map, but that hasn't happened yet.

I walk over to the beach and look at the endless, blue skies, the clear water, and the golden sand that glistens in the sunlight.

Splish! Splash! The spirited, silver waves leap up and land peacefully on the shores of the beach. I stand on the warm sand and enjoy the scene. The gentle breeze on the hot afternoon caresses my face. I find a comfy reading spot behind a large boat. I twist my curls as I start reading the next chapter of my mystery novel.

After ten minutes of reading, I look up from my book to enjoy the scenery again. To my right, there is a small hill with an ancient church on it. The church was built hundreds of years ago by the Portuguese, who had ruled Goa. The big clock outside the church *still* worked. We can hear the clock strike every hour from the beach and from the mansion.

I love attending prayers at the church, when we visit. People around the world don't always know that about 2% of Indians are Christians. That may seem like a small number, but that's over 28 million people. That's why some of us have names from the Bible and western names. Our religion is different, but our culture is very similar to all other Indians. You can't really tell us apart because we also look just like everyone else.

I go back to my book and turn the page to the next chapter. I hear Zach walking toward the beach. He is on his phone with a friend.

"I think I like her," he says.

*Bumblebees!! Zach has a crush.* I wonder who it is. My ears perk up as I try to hear what he was saying.

"Hmm, hmm, yeah I know," he says. "Yeah sounds good. Catch you later." Zach hangs up and then takes a couple of steps forward. He sees my hair sticking out from the side of the boat.

"Sammy, you little monkey. What did you hear?"

"Nothing..." I reply with a mischievous smile. Zach takes a handful of sand and flings it at me. I race back to the mansion giggling.

"Children, lunch is ready!" Georgy Uncle hollers from a distance. I run through the double-gated entrance toward the mansion and glance at the entrance gates as I go past them. Zach races behind me. The entrance has two statues of lions facing slightly toward each other, with one of their paws raised. It was a unique sculpture that was made when the mansion was built. The lions looked fierce and I remember being afraid of them when I was younger. I was even afraid of the shadows the lions made in the late afternoons.

I dust the silver sand off my blue shorts as I reach the outdoor table that Georgy Uncle has stacked with scrumptious food. Zach catches up and rolls his eyes at me. I can see that he is really mad. I grin back and giggle.

I look at the delicious lime-flavored roasted chicken and quickly gobble one of the grilled pepper shrimps.

"This is Yummylicious," I say to Georgy Uncle.

He smiles at me. "I love having you both over, you know." We finish lunch and clean up the patio table.

That afternoon, I stroll through the long hallway of portraits. I see a painting of a breathtaking sunset scene. Two coconut palms leaned toward each other, encompassing a beautiful scene of joyful waves. It looked like Bambolim beach. The sun just touched the waters and seems to be ready to set. The sky was reddish orange and the waters looked mystical.

Georgy Uncle joins me in the hallway. "I found this painting last month in the old attic," he says.

"Yes, I have never seen it before," I respond.

"Do you remember the stories I told you about Great Grand-Uncle Johnson Mathew? He painted this."

"Wow, he was a remarkable artist," I say softly.

"Yes, legend has it that he found a pirate treasure but hid it away. It's just a story. Your Papa and I have searched all over. We never found any treasure. Apacha told us the real treasure is to have a strong spirit and never give up."

"Apacha always gave advice that's not fun," I exclaim. *I wonder if I could find a real pirate's treasure.*

The painting had a rich, engraved, iron frame. There were two lions projecting out from the frame. They looked just like the lions on the entrance gates of the mansion. They faced each other and each had a paw raised.

The painting was slightly heavy. I notice tiny writing near some rocks on left side of the painting. I am not able to read it as it's really tiny. There was a signature on the right side of the portrait.

The day passes quickly and we go back to our rooms. We spend most of the week swimming, surfing and relaxing at the beach.

Today is the last day of our vacation, and Papa will pick us up tomorrow. We gather for breakfast. Georgy Uncle has prepared some garlic bread with chicken cutlets. Zach and I eat it up happily.

Georgy Uncle looks at us and then clears his throat. We look up at him.

"Children, this is probably going to be your last vacation here," he says, sipping his cup of green tea.

"What! That can't be true," exclaims Zach.

We look at each other in shock. "Why?" we say together.

"I am having money problems. It's getting hard for me to take care of such a huge mansion. There are some people who want to buy the mansion, and I am going to have to sell it. They plan to turn this place into a beach resort."

"That's awful," says Zach after an awkward silence.

"You can still visit the beach, but the mansion may no longer be around," Georgy Uncle says. He looks through the window onto the beach. He wipes a tear and adjusts his glasses.

"It's just not fair," I mumble.

We finish breakfast, and I walk sadly into the portrait hallway, sulking. I look around at all the portraits and the artifacts. I can't believe I won't get to spend time here again. I gaze at the beach painting again. It was so beautiful. Georgy Uncle enters the hallway and looks at me.

"I am sorry, Sammy. I know you love this mansion, but I have no way to save it."

I give him a hug. "I know you love this place too, Georgy Uncle. I am sorry you have to give it up."

"Sammy… you can have this painting. I know how much you love this beach and the mansion. You can keep this as a gift from me."

"Are you sure, Georgy Uncle?" I ask.

"Yes," he nods.

"Thank-you," I say. "I will treasure this precious gift always. Let's hope for some miracle! I hope we are able to save the mansion."

I take the painting to my room. That evening, I try to read the inscription again. What did Great Grand-Uncle Johnson Mathew want to tell us? *What if this is a clue to the treasure he found?*

My heart races a little as I take the painting to the library and place it carefully on Georgy Uncle's desk. I rummage through his shelves and find a magnifying glass. I pull up a stool, and peer at the inscription. I feel an exciting chill. It looks like it says

*'When they meet'.*

"I wonder what it means," I say aloud.

"What is it dear?" Georgy Uncle says as he enters the library.

"Look at this writing!" I shout excitedly to him.

11

Georgy Uncle looks at the inscription.

"It must be just something he scribbled," he says with a wave of his hand.

"I hadn't even noticed it. What can it mean anyway? It's too short of a message to be a clue," he shrugs. I spend the evening trying to figure out the phrase.

"Zach, who is he talking about? Is it a meeting between the pirates?"

"Go off to sleep, Miss Detective. You can figure it out tomorrow."

I give up and go to bed. I twist and turn, but I cannot sleep. I am sure it means something. The church clock strikes through the eerie night. I count twelve strikes. It's midnight. I better catch some sleep.

A lighthouse far away shines its light through the night sky. A bat strikes at my window. I jump out of my bed and look outside the window.

Crickets break the silence of the night. I feel a little chill down my spine. It seems like someone is in the room with me. *Who is it?*

I look at a portrait of Great Grand-Uncle Johnson in the hallway. The wind blows through an open window in the library. There is a stormy high tide at the beach. I can hear the waters whooshing against the rocks.

*Relax Sammy! There is no one out there,* I tell myself.

I look at the painting again. Am I holding the key to a big secret? Is Grand-Uncle Johnson trying to tell me something?

I close my bedroom door so I don't hear the eerie sounds again. I hug my soft teal pillow and bury myself in my cozy blanket as my eyes close. I think of the inscription again as I doze off to sleep. *'When they meet',* I wonder what it means.

# 2

# Fun on the Rooftop

Papa picks us up the next day. I give Georgy Uncle a long hug. I place the painting carefully in the passenger seat next to Papa, and force Zach to sit in the back with me.

We arrive at our apartment in Panaji city. I am sad about the mansion, but also excited about the mystery message in the ancient painting.

I hum a Bollywood tune as I gallop up the stairs to the rooftop. People think Bollywood is a place like Hollywood, but it only means the Indian movie industry. Most movies have very energetic and peppy songs.

I carry the beach painting with me, to explore it further. A gust of gentle breeze greets me with enthusiasm. At eleven stories high, my apartment building towers over many other buildings nearby. This rooftop or terrace as we call it, is shared by all the homes in our building. I look around, but at this time of the day there is no one else on the rooftop.

I roll up my frizzy dark hair into a bun and look at my reflection in the puddle of rainwater that had collected on the tiles. I love to admire my favorite blue sweatpants and green T-shirt. *They are so comfy.*

I plop on the concrete floor and start doodling with a small piece of chalk left over by some of the younger kids in the building. I write my real name on the floor in cursive, *'Samelda'.* Papa says my name means energetic, charismatic, ambitious and focused.

If only I had those qualities. Everyone thinks I am a strong girl, but I'm too scared to even ride a bike. If I hadn't broken my arm last summer, Papa could have taught me to ride. The year before, he was busy at work. And the years before, I was a scaredy-cat. I wish I did know to ride one though.

I text my BFF Layla; "Meet me at the rooftop. Have a mystery painting to show you."

Layla may have some ideas. Maybe we can figure out the meaning of the message together or even maybe find a pirate's treasure and save the mansion. *'When they meet', I wonder what the inscription means.*

I gaze at the road below. The busy scene of cars, buses, auto-rickshaws, bicyclists, and scooters greet me. The vehicles traversing the neighborhood honk with zeal. *I love this energy.* On the west side of the building, the coconut palms sway with the light breeze.

The endless, pristine, blue-green waters of the Indian Ocean glitter excitedly. The seagulls caw in a

17

distance. On a quiet night, you could even hear the sounds of the cheerful waves striking the rocks that line the waters. *I love Goa. I think it is the best place in India, or maybe even in the world.*

I wander toward the south end of the rooftop. This side of the terrace has a wall that is half as tall as me. Kids in our building loved to spy on homes in the opposite building by kneeling behind the short terrace wall and peeping over the edge. I peer across the wall to the balcony of my BFF Layla's apartment on the ninth floor of the opposite building.

The neat arrays of red and pink roses smile cheerfully. She's probably busy as she hasn't responded to my text yet. *I wonder if Charlie has arrived.* Charlie is Layla's cousin who lives in New York. He is in seventh grade, like me. Charlie visits Goa every summer.

Suddenly, Charlie steps out into the balcony. I freeze. He *has* landed. I duck behind the wall so he doesn't see my head bobbing above our terrace wall.

I slowly peep to get another glimpse. His silky, dark hair shines in the sunlight. He looks much taller than last year. And he is still cute. *Sigh!*

Charlie runs his fingers through his hair and looks at his reflection in the glass French doors of their balcony. He then poses for a selfie. He is still in love with himself! Just like last year!

I crawl back to the other side and go back to my painting. I listen to the background sounds, the gentle hum of the elevator, an occasional breeze that scatters a few dry leaves, and a solitary crow that starts cawing. All the sounds blend together as I look at the beautiful painting.

"Hi! Mr. Crow!" I say to the cawing crow.

I search through my pockets and find a cracker. I offer some cracker crumbs to Mr. Crow. It's almost 5

PM. I will take another quick look to see if Charlie is still there.

I crawl toward his side and peep above the wall. He's still there. He's still taking selfies on his phone. *Really, Charlie! Have you been doing this for the last 30 minutes?*

Suddenly Mr. Crow flies over to Charlie's side and circles around his head. Oh no! Mr. Crow decides to land some bird droppings on Charlie's silky hair. *Yikes!!*

Charlie looks in horror at Mr. Crow, and I start giggling. He looks up to the rooftop to see who was giggling. Oh no! *Hide!* I crawl to the back entrance and escape back to my spot, before I get caught.

I hear Layla's sandals slapping against the steps as she races up. I straighten my face so Layla can't tell I was laughing. Layla's cheeks are flushed with excitement when she bursts through the door.

"Sammy, I am so happy to see you. Show me your mystery painting."

I stutter a bit. "Hi Layla," I say. I try to hold back my laughter, but Charlie's horrified face keeps flashing before my eyes. Layla looks at me with a puzzled expression.

"Are you going to tell me about your mystery and step out of your daydream Ms. Sammy," she says with a snap of her fingers.

I clear my throat and wake up from my daze. I quickly fill Layla in on the past week.

"It was a bittersweet vacation. I'm heartbroken that I'm going to lose my vacation spot. But I also have a little mystery to solve."

"Sammy, I like the way you are thinking. Thanks to all those mystery books you read," Layla says.

"Yes, but we need to figure out the meaning of the message on the painting," I reply.

"What do we do next?" Layla asks.

"I don't know," I laugh. "But, I am sure the message means something. We need to figure it out and I am super excited about that."

# 3

# Home Sweet Home

It's almost 7 PM. It's time for the highlight of the day. The mighty sun is about to set, and the azure sky has streaks of carrot-orange, ruby, pink, and gold. The clouds make patterns, and the sun gradually sinks into the waters.

"It is beautiful, isn't it?" Layla says dreamily.

"Absolutely, it never fails to inspire!" I respond.

"We are lucky to be able to see this beautiful sunset every day," Layla adds.

"Yes, each day the scene seems to be different and the patterns seem to change," I reply.

I imagine the message from the painting floating in the sky, *'When they meet'*. The imaginary message drifts through the clouds. What could it mean?

Several children race to play on the rooftop. Their scuffling and laughter wake me up from my daydream. A little boy switches on the lights of the towering lamppost on the terrace. Yellow light floods the area.

The sky turned darker and the colors change to shades of crimson and gray. It is dusk now and the sun sets gracefully. The cheerful moon greets us on the other side of the terrace.

The elevator dings and Charlie walks on to the rooftop. My heart skips a beat as I see his familiar face.

"How long is he here for?" I ask Layla.

"Two more weeks," Layla replies.

Charlie joins a couple of other boys on the corner. He pretends like he doesn't see me.

"Your cousin is such a snob," I tell Layla.

"He is just shy. Why don't you go and say hi?" she says.

"Yeah, I mean he does know me. He could at least look up," I reply.

I see Layla smile from the corner of my eye, but I pretend not to notice.

I look away quickly, so she doesn't see me blush. *I'm not going to admit I like him, even if she is my BFF.*

A delightful breeze blows from the beach on the west side and my hair flies in a whimsical manner. The sky lights up with shining stars. Shivering slightly in the evening chill, I turn to leave.

"I'll see you later, Layla. Think about the inscription okay?"

"Okay, I'll see you tomorrow," she says.

I pick up the painting with both hands and carefully go down the stairs from the rooftop, toward my apartment.

The smell of fried fish wafts from my home. I pop my head into the kitchen to greet Papa, who is tossing the salad and Mamma who carefully scoops fried fish from the hot coconut oil.

Papa is an executive at the Indian division of a huge multinational company. He is also a total foodie. He enjoys cooking with Mamma just as much as he enjoys leading innovations at work.

"Hey! Mamma, the kingfish smells great. You make the best fish fry in all of Goa."

"Thanks dear!" Mamma replies with a smile.

Zach is in the family room with his head buried in a math book.

I wish I had the patience to study like him, but math is hard and there were too many superhero

26

shows to watch. I love watching 'The Flash' & 'Supergirl'. I could watch them a hundred times. If only Mamma would let me watch TV all day.

I go to my room and put the painting carefully on my table. I gaze at the painting for a little. Suddenly, I have that familiar feeling again.

Is the painting trying to tell me something? Is there a secret it is hiding? This time I am not afraid... but I can't help but wonder.

*It feels like I'm not alone.*

I sigh and wrap the painting in some paper tissue, so it does not get dusty. I place it carefully in my bookshelf. I will ask Papa to help me hang it on my wall when he can.

I stare at my ceiling as I lay down in bed at night. How can I save my mansion? Should I enroll in Bollywood dance classes this summer? Would I be laughed at because I am a little awkward at dancing?

Slowly I drift off to sleep. I can see myself dancing. I am on a stage with lotus flowers. Beautiful Bollywood music fills the air.

Then a medley of music beats from traditional Indian instruments like sitars and tablas can be heard. There seems to be a fragrance of jasmine as well. I dance easily to the peppy music.

Suddenly, the scene shifts to Bambolim beach and the dance continues. The clouds seem happy; the coconut trees are swaying, even the waves seem joyful too.

I look up to see my dance partner. He appears hazy at first. Then his face becomes clear.

It's Robbie Kapoor, the famous, young Indian film star. His wavy, black hair flies in the wind and his brown eyes look at me. Everyone cheers. I smile at the scene.

How much more awesome can it get? Robbie Kapoor dancing to Bollywood music! With me on the golden sands of Bambolim beach!

Goa's beaches are beautiful indeed. Home sweet home! I never want to live anywhere else.

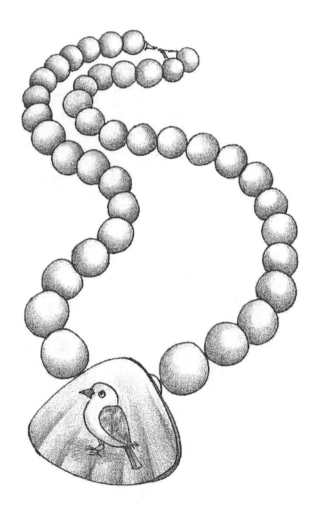

# 4

# An Unexpected Discovery

A yoga session is on TV as I join my family for breakfast. Papa picks up the remote and switches the TV off. I look up at his face. I can't tell if he is excited or tense.

"Zach and Sammy, we have some news to share with you. I have been offered a promotion to head our Analytics division in the United States of America! Mamma and I have talked about it, and we are very thrilled. It's an opportunity of a lifetime that we don't want to turn down."

We look at each other in shock.

"What! We don't want to move," Zach says in alarm.

"What are you guys thinking? School is awesome here. Goa is beautiful. What about our friends?" I protest.

"Children, America has more opportunities than here. They have the best universities and better jobs too. We thought you both would be excited!"

"No! Why move?" I start sobbing. "It's a bad thing we are losing the mansion and now this? I can't lose my friends, my home and my vacation spot all at once."

"Children, look at the positive side. It would be extremely hard for you to gain admission to Harvard and MIT as an international student. It would be easier if you were educated there. If we move now, the sky is the limit."

"But I don't want to go to Harvard," I protest. "I will just study at Goa College of Engineering."

"Sammy, I think I would like to study at an Ivy League college," Zach chimes in. "Papa does have a point!"

"Traitor, huh Zach you are impossible! Why do you always have to be perfect? This is horrible," I cry out.

Papa interrupts me, "It's a good thing it's summer break now. You will be starting at a new school in Reston, Virginia in the fall. Sammy, I know this seems hard, but this is best for the family and for you. You will thank us one day for this tough choice."

"No way, I don't want to leave this home or my friends." I shove back my chair and bolt into my room. I slam my door and fling myself on my bed and cry till my eyes are puffy and red. The whole day seems gloomy. I surf through TV channels, slumped on the couch. Susheela bai, our maid, hands me a cup of Indian chocolate milk.

I look up at her and say, "Shukriya," which means thank-you in Hindi. I've heard maids are not common in America. I wonder what life would be like without a maid. *Would I have to help Mamma with the dishes?*

A delicious aroma of chickpea flour–dipped, fried onions and potatoes called 'bhajis', wafts from my neighbor's home.

A few minutes later, my eight-year-old neighbor knocks at our open door and hands me a platter of the delicious bhajis with a smile.

I put the plate in the kitchen and take a bite of the salty, crunchy onions. Mamma will probably make her famous Rose cookies tomorrow and ask me to return the plate.

I wonder what food the neighbors in the America would share with us. Do neighbors even share food there? Gosh! We are going to miss our neighborhood. *Why do my parents think this is a great idea?*

That evening, I text Layla, "Meet me at the rooftop in 10?" I grab a big pack of chocolate biscuits and run up the stairs.

The hill is now lit with yellow bulb lights in the smaller homes and silver-white light in the buildings. It seems like a giant necklace of gold and platinum. The downtown area is still bright with the headlights of the vehicles.

"I don't want to ever leave this rooftop and this beauty. We have a good life here," I mumble.

Layla comes over and I break the news. She looks sad. She remains quiet for a few minutes and then gives me a smile and a hug.

"Well, it's not as bad as you think, Sammy," she says. "Charlie surely likes it there. The schools don't have uniforms. They don't have two hour exams like us. Life is easier there. The multi-storied malls are beautiful. The streets are clean. You will like it there. I will miss you terribly, but I am actually happy for you."

"Yeah and I will miss my home and everyone here," I sigh.

"But you are going to the *United States of America*. Virginia is only a four hour drive from New York."

"So?" I ask.

"Your family may visit Charlie's family when you go to see the Statue of Liberty," she teases with a grin.

"Stop, Layla... I am so worried here and you find this time to be funny!"

"Oh, come on; admit it! You really like him."

"No, I don't," I say. "He is annoying. He won't even talk to me. Why would I like him?" I lie, avoiding her eyes.

Layla smiles, "You are going to be just fine Ms. Sammy. I wish my family was moving to America."

I sigh and give her a hug. From the rooftop, we watch the vehicles on the road below, for a little while.

"It's a little chilly today. Do you want to hang out at my house?" I ask.

"Sure, let's go," she replies.

We enter my room and Layla looks through my bookshelf. "You have so many mystery novels, Sammy."

"Yes, but I can't solve my own real life mystery," I reply. "I have no idea what this message from the painting means," I grumble.

I place the painting on my bed and examine the frame. Layla continues to look through my books. Suddenly I feel my heart beating a little faster.

"Layla, what if these lion paws on the frame are supposed to meet?" I ask in excitement.

"Try it," she suggests and comes over to look at the frame.

I tug at the lion's paw and it does not budge. I try once more and one of the metal lions shifts slightly to the left closer to the other lion.

"Whoa," Layla exclaims.

I tug at it once more but it seems stuck.

"It's probably really rusty inside," I say.

"Yeah…after all it is a few hundred years old." Layla responds.

Gently I am able to slide the lion to the left and the stretched paws of both lions meet.

"Layla, there seems to be a small compartment in the frame that I can see now, after moving the lion to the left."

"Goodness! Is there anything in it?" Layla asks excitedly, trying to get a better look over my shoulder.

"Looking," I reply. A million thoughts fill my

head. What could be in it? I can't believe we may have found a treasure.

I hold my breath and run my fingers inside the compartment and feel something. I peer eagerly in and gently remove an exquisite pearl necklace with an amulet made of white coral. A beautiful sparrow was carved onto the amulet.

"It's beautiful!" Layla utters.

"Probably not very precious," I reply. "It's not going to save the mansion!"

"Yes, I was expecting something precious too," Layla responds.

"This may have been made with the pearls and corals off the Bambolim shore itself," I say, slumping on my bed with disappointment.

I look at Layla with a frown. "I am a little upset that our mystery ended with a boring climax."

"Yes, I'm sorry this didn't solve your mansion problem Sammy," Layla says.

"This has turned out to be a rather pointless hunt. I could wear the necklace with my white skirt but I wasn't exactly looking for fashion accessories in the painting," I complain.

"Don't fret Sammy," Layla says. "Perhaps, the amulet has some magic."

"Abracadabra, what can you do?" I ask the amulet.

"There has to be something special if your Great Grand-Uncle hid it in this painting," Layla says.

"What do you mean?" I reply.

"I am sure it is a magic necklace. You just need to figure out how to make it work."

"Okay," I reply.

"Maybe you need to wear it," Layla says.

"Don't raise my hopes, Layla," I reply. I put the necklace on but nothing happens.

"Hmm, maybe there is a secret chant?" I ask.

"Well, how do we find that now?" Layla replies.

I guess, I will figure out one day how to make this magic work," I laugh.

# 5

# Hello America!

The next few weeks pass by quickly. We finish packing and say our goodbyes to our friends and neighbors. All our furniture has already shipped on a cargo ship.

Three cars full of neighbors and friends come to drop us off at the airport. A bunch of kids, Layla, Reshma, Rhianna, Shilpa, Haley, Allan, along with many adults, Aunty Preethy, Uncle Rahul, Uncle Raj, Aunty Veena, Aunty Cini and others, come to see us off. The adults are friends of my parents but we call them Aunty and Uncle, even if they are not relatives.

Layla's Grandma, Amma has made her famous lemon rice for us to eat on the flight. Papa protests and explains to her that the security guards won't let us carry any food. But, she insists we should either try to convince them or eat it right before boarding.

Everyone is thrilled about us migrating to America. They chitter-chatter and make such a ruckus, that the security guards raise their eyebrows at us.

With all the excited chatter, I hope the guards don't kick us out of the airport. I understand the love, but I don't understand all the excitement, when I am losing everything I have. I smile politely at everyone, because Papa says we must never forget our manners.

Three hours later, we board our flight. I've only been on short plane rides, and this is the first time I am travelling outside India. I wonder what it would be like to be on a plane for eighteen hours. I am amazed there are so many Bollywood movies to choose from on the flight. I watch a lot of movies.

The food is yummy on the flight. Amma surely shouldn't have bothered with the lemon rice, which we had to gobble up before security check-in. Mamma says we should not waste food. But, now I am so full with all the eating.

I hope my beach painting is safe in my check-in luggage. I can't believe the mansion will be sold in six months. I hold on to my coral amulet. I doze off in my seat and see weird dreams that I can't seem to remember when I wake up.

We arrive at Dulles airport in Virginia. We go through a long immigration line, and my parents answer some questions. My Papa has a work visa. I still don't understand why my parents needed to leave their comfortable lives back in India.

We arrive at our new townhome. All the townhomes on our street look identical. Our home is bigger than our apartment home in India, because we have a basement. But the bedrooms are much smaller than our rooms in India. The walls are so thin you can almost hear the neighbors. We have to climb a lot of stairs as our bedrooms are on the top level.

A few days pass and I start adjusting to the new home. Zach will be in high school, and I will be in middle school. In India, we both would have been in the same school till tenth grade. Zach is totally chill about going to a new school. I know Zach will have no problem making friends. He is the popular kind. I know I would have more trouble.

Papa loves his new job. Mamma's visa does not allow her to take a job. Mamma was an advertising executive in Goa for ten years. I am a little surprised that she agreed to migrate on a visa that would not allow her to work. She is having a hard time managing all the chores with no maid. But she seems happy. It's a good thing Papa helps out. I should help her too, but dishes and chores are boring!

School starts in two weeks. I take my placement tests, and we get ready. Today we are visiting my school. As Papa drives us to the school, I look out the window and gaze at the clean streets and orderly traffic. How boring! No honking, no energy on the roads.

We pull in to the parking lot and I am surprised how big the school is. Papa scans his ID at the door and we enter in. There is a lot more security at schools here than in India. I look in amazement at the huge hallway, the wall decorations and the tall ceilings.

The counselor, Ms. Gabe greets us at the school office and gives us visitor passes. She shows us the locker room and the classrooms. We did not have lockers in my earlier school in India. We also didn't have different classrooms for each subject.

Ms. Gabe continues to explain how the classes work. I am astonished that I have to run to different classes for each subject, with just few minutes to rush to the locker and switch binders. It was so much easier in India, where we would just sit in a class and all the teachers would come to us. We had about 40 students per class and had the same classmates throughout the year. Here, we had only about 25 students per class but nearly 300 students in each grade. I would have different classmates in each of my classes. How do you make friends in middle school if you hardly get to see the same classmates? I try to grasp all of this information from Ms. Gabe, and it still seems hard to understand all of it.

Soon the first day of school arrives. I am nervous about the big day. I get off the school bus and enter the school. I almost forget where the 7th grade locker room is. I track it down and try to remember the instructions. Most of the kids in 7th grade know each other, because they were together in school for years. They laugh and talk and I feel almost invisible.

I find my way to the first classroom and reach in time. The teachers are very helpful and make sure I understand the school rules. The classrooms are very bright and cheerful, but I don't feel very cheerful in a room full of classmates, I don't know.

The bell rings for lunch. I enter the huge cafeteria. I have a $5.00 bill, that Mamma gave me this morning and stand in the line to order lunch. I buy some chicken nuggets with broccoli, a chocolate chip cookie and milk. I find a spot at an empty table and sit down.

No one comes to join me at my table and I finish my lunch alone. I'm a little afraid to talk to the other kids. I wonder if they will understand my Indian accent. Would they think I am weird?

The day ends quickly. I use the instructions given by my teacher, to make sure I don't get lost on my way to my school bus. I hold the paper in hand and look at the long line of identical yellow buses. I find the right one and sit quietly at a window seat. No one comes to sit near me.

I reach my bus-stop after a short ride. Zach's high school bus arrives a little later at the same bus-stop. Kids get off the bus and walk in different directions to their own homes. A few kids who know each other wave and talk. But no one looks at me or acknowledges me. I walk home quietly. How different this is from my noisy, packed bus ride in India. We would be yelling and screaming and having so much fun.

That afternoon Mamma asks me, "How was your day?"

"It was fine," I reply.

It wasn't a good day at all. I feel a tear swell up in my eye, but I don't let Mamma see that. I hate school. I miss my friends and my school in Goa. I miss my BFF Layla. I feel like a bird that has been captured from the sky and has forgotten how to fly.

# 6

# The Sparkly Surprise

I go to my bedroom and look outside my window. The neat arrays of identical townhouses look back at me. We don't know any of our neighbors. We haven't even seen most of them, and it has been three weeks since we moved in. Occasionally I see people biking on the sidewalk, but I don't even know if they are from our community or passing by to the next neighborhood.

Each day, my ride on the school bus is the same. I sit all by myself. Another week passes by, and today is Friday. I am in an after-school drama activity for the Community Fall festival, as a backstage helper. I signed up as a backstage helper because I didn't think I would get picked for anything else. Our school is preparing for a pantomime, which is a musical stage production with different types of arts.

There is a ballet section in which Julia, the most popular ballet dancer in seventh grade is performing. I look around at all the kids in the drama club. Why did twelve year-olds have to dress like they were sixteen? Everyone seemed to be in stylish jeans and pretty tops. Many had their hair all set. Two of Julia's friends, Alicia and Megan even seemed to have some makeup on today. I watch the performers as I stand backstage. Some eighth graders finish their routine and walk out of the stage.

"Move out of the way," sneers one of them.

"So...So... Sorry," I stutter and get out of their way. I look back on stage. Julia pulls herself up and starts her routine.

52

She hoists herself on a single foot and does an easy cartwheel. She seems to be light as a feather. Her hair is tied up in a tight bun. Her face is grim with a determined look. She flips and then lands on a single foot. She looks like a swan. No wonder she is popular.

Alicia and Megan are part of the dance with Julia. I don't know the rest of the girls. They stretch and stand on their toes and swirl across the floor. Everyone applauds their performance.

It looks effortless, but clearly they have had several years of rigorous training. Julia is the leader at the game. I definitely don't think I should try speaking to her or Alicia or Megan.

There's another dance sequence that six other girls are presenting. It's one of my favorite songs. If only I had gone to dance classes as a kid, I might have been able to participate at the very least. Of course, I would look great dancing if I was fashionably dressed. The only thing I can wear comfortably to school is loose T-shirts and sweatpants, and that is *not* how the popular girls dress!

I wish I was good at something. But I am terrified just with the thought of being on stage. What if I forget my lines? What if I stutter?

Exercise could help me be more athletic, but I don't want to exercise either. What I really want is another cookie from the snacks table. I hope nobody noticed; I ate four of the cookies at the rehearsal today. Sugar makes me forget all my troubles.

A group of boys from seventh grade enter, and talk to the dancers. A tall boy, named Ryan from my bus-stop is with the group. He is in my math class too, but I've never even tried to say hi to him so far.

The boys get along so well with Alicia and Megan. Boys are annoying. Boys always seem to like the pretty girls. I dislike boys... except Charlie of course.

I wonder what Charlie is up to in New York. He is cute, but the next time I see him, I wish he would just talk to me!

Would my parents want to visit his family when we go to see the Statue of Liberty? I smile thinking of Layla trying to tease me about that. It would be awkward if he still doesn't speak to me. Maybe I should start talking to him and jabber away. I laugh aloud, thinking how confused he would be with my new talkativeness.

There are several other kids in my classes that I want to speak to, but I am too afraid to say hi. Isn't there one thing I can be truly good at? If only I had one good friend here. Just one! What a lonely life I had.

That night I sit at my bed unable to fall asleep. I miss my home, my old school, my BFF and my country. I remember all the good times and I feel a tear fall down my cheek. Soon another one rolls down and I start sniffling. I am annoyed that I cry so easily and try to wipe off my salty tears. I really don't want to wake my parents. They would be so disappointed to see me cry.

I say a little prayer for strength. I look around and the familiar feeling returns. The same feeling I had when I first got the painting. The feeling I felt in my apartment building in Goa. Like someone is in the room. But I am not scared. It seems exciting!

*Who is it?* I think out aloud.

I absentmindedly hold on to the coral amulet with both my hands and suddenly there is a cool breeze. Why is there a breeze, when my windows are closed?

Suddenly there is a spark of purple light and a whoosh sound.

"Whoa!" I exclaim. The amulet turns into a real miniature white sparrow and appears in front of me. I shriek in disbelief.

The sparrow shines like sunlight through a prism, in my dark room. A rainbow of lights, sparkle around it, creating the most beautiful sight I had ever seen.

The sparkling sparrow says, "Hello Sammy."

"Huh, you talk?" I ask and my eyes widen. Was I dreaming? Is this bird really talking to me? I pinch myself a few times.

The sparrow nods. "Yes, I do talk."

"You are a talking sparrow from an amulet? What an amazing surprise! You must be magical?" I exclaim in wonder.

"Yes, when your hands meet on the amulet, the magic is invoked. That's what your uncle also meant when he wrote '*When they meet*'. But, I only come when you really need me."

I look in awe at this most beautiful bird.

"Layla *had* said I needed to figure out how to make the amulet work," I say.

57

The sparkling sparrow continues, "Yes, the amulet is 400 years old and has the magic of the ocean in it."

"Can you move us back to India? My parent's plan of migrating to America isn't exactly working out for me," I say.

"No, I can't make major changes like that. But, I can help you with your new life here. You cannot tell anyone about me, not just yet," the sparrow says.

"Okay, my magical friend!" I respond.

"You are a special girl. You have powers that you do not know about. You can easily handle the challenges ahead of you," the mystical sparrow says.

"Hmm…" I say. I am not fully convinced if this sparrow is real, but I nod.

Then the sparrow pauses and whispers, *"I may be able to even help you with a little magic here and there."*

# 7

# My Little Friend

The next morning, I find it really hard to wake up. I am late and almost miss the bus!

*Did I dream about the sparrow?* Was she real?

I keep thinking about my magical friend. That night, I put both my hands again on the amulet and nothing happens. Well, she did say she would come only when I really needed her. I sleep off.

It's the next day and I have a math test. I didn't study much, but I hope I do well. The test concludes and ten minutes later we get our scores.

I get 3 out of 20! My eyes tear up and I quickly rub my eyes, before tears trickles down my cheek. I can't let anyone in class see me cry!

How do I tell Mamma about my test score? I get off the bus and walk quietly with my head down. I see Ryan, the boy from my math class, but I ignore him.

That night, I bury my face in my hands and say a little prayer. I lie down on my bed and wonder what to do. Now that I think of it, I may have dreamt of the sparkling sparrow. I don't think she is real. I am too different than everyone else. I don't like my life.

I hold on to my amulet and close my eyes.

And there she was. A flash of light and my sparkling friend comes to visit me again.

"Hello Sammy, how can I help you today?"

"You are real! I thought I saw you in a dream. Where have you been? I have been waiting for you!"

"I only come when you really need me," she replies.

"You promised you would help me... with magic? The best thing would be if you could move us back to India."

"Sammy, I'm sorry. You know I can't change things like that. But, I can solve one problem of yours today."

"Okay... nobody talks to me at school. Rather I don't talk to anyone."

The sparrow says, "I will cast a spell on you to make a new friend tomorrow. You just need to make a genuine effort to be nice to people."

"But, I'm nervous. What if they don't like me? What if they think I am weird?" I reply.

"You have to believe good things will happen, Sammy. You have to be ready to take risks. My magic spell will help you."

"Is this spell actually going to work, my little friend?" I say.

"If you don't believe in my magic, it won't work. Write it down and believe in it. You won't see me, but I will be watching over you."

"Okay," I reply. "Like a guardian angel or a fairy god mother?"

"Well, I can't turn a pumpkin into a carriage," she laughs. "You can think of me as a special friend. But you need to do your part as well, so my magic can work."

She says a few words that I don't understand, and a ray of yellow light falls on me. I widen my eyes in surprise. And poof ...she disappears!

*What did she say again? Write down what I want?*

I take a little notebook from my messy table and write on it. "I am going to make a new friend tomorrow."

Oh, this is impossible! I put my pencil back on my table. What magic is this? This is just nonsense. I'm dreaming with my eyes wide open.

The next morning, I can't stop thinking of the sparrow's words. Will I make a new friend today? She said I must take risks and make a genuine effort.

My morning classes go by quickly. At lunch, I take a deep breath and smile at a girl sitting alone, eating her lunch. I know she is in history class with me.

"Hi, I am Sammy," I say. The girl looks up at me and smiles.

"My name is Kim. Would you like to sit with me for lunch?"

"Yeah," I say excitedly. I hadn't thought it would be this easy.

"I came from India last month," I tell Kim.

"Okay. My family is from Korea but I was born here. What do you like to do in your free time?"

I want to say, I listen to Bollywood songs but I'm not sure if she would know what it means. I think of my next favorite thing.

"I like 'The Flash'," I reply.

"Wow, that's my favorite show too," she says.

I feel a shiver of excitement. I was finally speaking to someone at school. She seemed to understand my English. We talk and talk about 'The Flash'. Sometimes, I have to repeat what I say, but she doesn't seem to mind. My sparrow friend was right. I just needed to work on being nice to others.

That afternoon, I am excited about talking to more kids. I am going to try to speak more. Maybe I will start liking this new school!

I get on the bus and see Julia, the popular ballet dancer. She is in my English class, so she probably knows me. I take a deep breath to say hi, but she is busy on her phone and ignores me. She doesn't look up.

I turn away a little embarrassed, to an empty seat. That didn't go exactly as I had planned. I hope no one saw me try to talk to her. Jeez!

I get off the bus and start walking home. Zach's high school bus has arrived a little early today. I see Zach laugh and talk to some boys at the bus-stop. How does he do it? How is he so comfortable talking to new kids who are so different than him?

I see Ryan besides Zach's group. Ryan starts walking toward me and away from the group. "Okay, I am going to say hello this time," I say to myself.

I see him continue to walk toward me and I open my mouth to say 'hi', but before I can speak, I freeze. I quickly turn around and start walking fast toward my home. Yikes, maybe tomorrow!

I try to listen to my sparrow friend's voice in my head, but I am not the confident type. Talking to boys is a lot harder than talking to girls. I will keep working on it, little by little.

The next day, I decide I am not going to give up. I am going to try again. My sparrow friend's voice echoes in my mind. "Be nice, take risks."

I should put my fear aside and talk to more kids. Maybe they will accept my culture. Maybe they won't roll their eyes at my Indian accent.

I enter my science class. I am on a project with Sheba and Becky. They are nice to me. I try to talk more to them. Sometimes I don't fully understand their jokes, but that's okay. They don't seem to mind how different I am.

My next class is math. I have another test today and I'm nervous about it. I will get the test scores at the end of the class.

Gosh! I got 2 out of 10. What is going on?

I'm pretty sure I am not going to be able to keep this away from Mamma for long. She can login to her parent account and view this online anyway.

In the evening, Mamma has made some yummy chicken puffs. I happily bite into it but I'm still wondering how to tell Mamma about my math disasters. I look at her face and she seems to be in a good mood. Slowly, I gather enough courage…

"Mamma, I got a bad score in my math tests. I'm sorry."

I expect her to yell, but she responds in a calm voice. "Sammy, I know you can do better. I know this move has been tough on you. Why don't you work with Zach on your math?"

*Did she just ask me to work with Zach? No way!*

"Yeah okay," I reply. I know I am not going to ask Zach to help. He is just going to tease me and say I am annoying.

I go back to my room. I wish my sparrow friend could help me with big acts of magic. It would be cool if she could make me popular or a great math whiz.

How awesome it would be, if she could save the mansion, or magically teach me to ride a bike!

I look at the stack of Girl Scout cookies, we bought in the parking lot. I will just eat four more. What difference will it make? I am too awkward to learn to dance. I can't ride a bike and I am too dumb for math.

I look at my favorite painting. I wish I could go back to Bambolim beach. I look at the writing again, *'When they meet'*.

I quickly put on my amulet and hold both my hands on the sparrow's picture. At first nothing happens. I close my eyes and long for my magical sparrow friend to arrive.

Suddenly, there is a cool gust of wind again, a little flash of light and there she was.

"Hello Sammy!"

"There you are! I really need your help!"

"Tell me what you need."

68

"I want to go back to Goa."

"I'm sorry Sammy. I've told you already. I have just a little bit of magic. I can't make big changes like that. But I can help you with little things. Did my spell on you work? Were you able to make a new friend? "

"Hmm… yeah," I say. "Kim talks to me, but I don't have a BFF. I am still afraid to talk to most of the other kids."

The mystical sparrow looks at me and says, *"Sammy, be a good friend to others and you will make plenty of friends. "*

I nod and bite my lower lip. "Okay, what do you mean?"

"Keep working on it," the sparrow says. "When you make a friend, you feel happy…but remember you are also helping someone else by being *their* friend. Be a great friend to others. Be nice and helpful."

"Hmm… okay," I say.

"What else do you need?" the sparrow asks.

"Hmm... can you please help me score better in math," I ask earnestly, looking at her in the eye.

"Deal, I am going to cast a spell on you. I will help you remember everything you study. But first you have to do your part. You have to study and understand the concepts," she says.

"Okay... how?" I ask, narrowing my eyes.

"Maybe, you can ask Zach to help you? It won't be as bad as you think. I will do my part of the magic, by casting my spell."

I nod. "Okay... if you say so."

"Sammy, never be embarrassed to fail. We must keep on trying to achieve whatever we want. We all deserve to be happy. Don't hold yourself back. Each one of us was made to be successful!"

"I guess... I can try asking him," I say softly.

The magical sparrow says some more words I don't understand again and a yellow light falls on me, one more time! *She has cast another spell on me.* Then she vanishes.

*Wow! Was that for real?* I better do my part. Let me see if Zach is still awake. I go out of my room into the hallway. Zach's room is still partly open and his light is on. I knock at his door with my math book in hand. Zach has his headphones on with some music.

I am going to keep my pride aside. Maybe Zach can actually help me. With the spell, perhaps I will remember everything I study.

"Zach!" I holler. He looks at me with a puzzled expression. I show him my math book. He hits the pause button and puts the headphones around his neck.

"What's up Sammy?"

"Zach, do you think you could tutor me a little in math?" I chew my pencil a little, ready for him to snicker and mock me. I hope my sparrow friend is right and Zach *can* help me.

71

"Oh, I thought you'd never ask. You know I love math. I'd be happy to teach you."

I look at him in shock. *It can't be this easy.*

And there it comes...

"But," he pauses, "you have to do my laundry in return."

"Spinach in my teeth...! You are so annoying! Fine!!! " I agree.

Zach was indeed a genius at math and at teaching. He quickly revises all the math concepts that I kept getting wrong. Then he shares some tutorials on his Chromebook while he continues to work on his practice books. I look at the practice books he is working on. They are all for 9th grade. *They look very familiar.*

Gosh! I have the same practice books for 7th grade that Mamma ordered for me online. I can't remember where I stuffed them in my room. I don't think I even opened them. They are probably still in a box under my bed. I should look for them!

The online tutorials were really helpful, and I ask Zach for help when I am stuck. I don't realize how time passes by quickly and its 11PM. I yawn.

"Let's do the rest tomorrow," he says.

"Okay," I say picking up my stuff.

If only I had realized this sooner and kept my pride aside, maybe I wouldn't have had to struggle so much at math.

Zach may be annoying at other times but he was really good at teaching math. I have another test in 2 weeks. *I wonder if my sparrow friend's spell will work.*

# 8

# Double Whammy!

"Sammy! Sammy!" I hear someone calling out, but I slip again from the edge of a cliff. It seems like it's my dream, but this time it's for real! I try to grasp a branch, but it slips through my fingers. I keep falling down the same vast valley. "Help...! Help...!" I try to move my hand but I can't.

Suddenly I wake up with a startle. It *was* a dream after all! What is this horrible dream I keep having?

It is almost 4 AM. I toss and turn and finally my alarm rings. Yikes! Now I'll be sleepy in class!

After school, in the evening, I sit at my study table and do my homework. I see a bunch of kindergartners zoom by on their bikes. American kids enjoy biking a lot. The roads in India are too busy for bikes, so it isn't that important. Well, that's one more reason, why I shouldn't be here in the first place. I can't ride a bike, and I am too old for training wheels. Everyone learns to ride when they are six and seven years old in America, and I am twelve already!

The next day, Kim is out from school. I am alone at lunch. I still don't have anyone to sit with me on the bus ride back home as well. I miss Layla and all my friends back in India. I remember singing Bollywood songs in the bus and talking and laughing. I wish my sparrow friend could do a lot more magic. I try to follow all the advice she has given me, but it is still hard to make friends.

I reach home and am back at my study table finishing my homework.

A little later, I hear Papa talking enthusiastically at the dining table. He is back from work. I run down the stairs to greet Papa. I can smell some mouth-watering tacos from the nearby fast food store. I do appreciate how quickly you can buy fast food at almost every corner in America. I reach the bottom of the stairs, and my smile quickly turns into a frown. Papa was standing with a new purple bike. It was shiny and …it had training wheels!!!

Papa says, "Sammy, check out this new bike I got you."

"Oh Papa, I am too big for training wheels."

"Sammy, don't worry. In America, kids like to ride bikes. You will learn soon enough."

Papa was so excited, I couldn't break his heart. "Let's go to the community park," he says. How could I tell him how afraid I was?

"Sammy, maybe we can go to Little Park. You decide which park you want to go to," Papa says.

"I don't want to go to any park today," I reply.

He looks at me in surprise, "Why not?"

"I have a lot of homework," I fib.

"Come on, Sammy. Don't be a stick in the mud," Papa calls, "let's have some fun."

"Okay, let's go over the weekend Papa," I reply and give him a hug and run to my bedroom.

*I can make up some excuse when the weekend is here.*

I see some more kindergartners zoom by on bikes outside my bedroom window. I am probably the only one in school who hasn't learned to ride a bike.

I open my books. Let me finish the problems that Zach asked me to focus on. Maybe, I can forget about this gift from Papa. I really don't want to embarrass myself in the park. I dislike training wheels! *I am too big for them, and everyone will look at me.*

And then in the evening after dinner, there was another surprise in store for me. Today seems like a really bad day!

"Sammy, I know how much you love watching Bollywood movies and dances," Mamma says.

"Huh! What about it?" I ask.

"I have registered you for dance classes at Bolly Mania"

"Why...?" I ask in dismay.

"To learn dance?" she narrows her eyebrows and gives me a puzzled look. "Don't you love Bollywood dances?"

She continues, "It's once a week on Thursdays at 6.30 PM. I paid for 12 classes as they had a promotion. Can you call them and ask them about dress code?"

"What...! No Mamma! You paid already? Why didn't you ask me? I am too awkward to dance."

"Oh Sammy, that is nonsense. You've always loved dancing. I did not even think you would be upset. It will be fun for you."

"No…. Mamma, you should have at least asked me?" I protest.

"Sammy, please don't make excuses for everything. You don't have to be a great dancer to enjoy dance. It will also keep you in touch with our culture. Just try it out, and we can cancel if you don't like it… okay?"

"Okay!" I reply. I knew I would hate it!

Mamma never cancels any class once we enroll. She just keeps saying she will cancel.

I go back to my room. I am really angry and upset. *Why do parents think they always know best?*

I take my coral amulet and try to hold it so I can talk to my sparrow friend. But nothing happens. I wonder where she is or how I could reach her when I want to talk to her. Maybe she won't come when I am angry.

I look at my painting. It helps me relax and forget all my troubles. Great Grand-Uncle Johnson, were you thinking of something more when you wrote the inscription? Is a bigger secret in the inscription? When who meet? Were they pirates? Was it a lady you loved?

My phone buzzes, interrupting my thoughts. It's Layla. *Thank goodness for phones.* I have so much to tell her. We video chat each other and quickly catch up. I whisper so my parents can't hear me.

"Layla, just when I thought my life couldn't get worse, Papa gets me a baby bike and Mamma wants me to go for dance lessons. What a double whammy!"

"I'm sorry, girl!" Layla says.

"Zach has an A+ in math. I am too old to ride a bike; I still don't have a BFF."

"Hang in there girl," says Layla. "Tomorrow will be a new day."

# 9

# Has the magic begun?

The next morning as I walk toward my bus-stop, I suddenly see my sparrow friend perched above the Stop sign.

She sparkles in the daylight almost like a shining star. She was delicate and fascinating.

"How did you get here?" I whisper.

"I'm magical. You have released me from the amulet, so I can actually appear on my own free will. Sometimes you need to invoke the magic, but at times I will just show up, " she says with a smile.

"Okay… then why didn't you appear last night? I had so much to tell you. Do you know about the baby bike and the dance lessons?" I ask.

"Yes, I won't appear when you are angry. We can deal with those problems one by one," she replies.

"Okay, what is your plan for today?" I say with a grin.

"I'm here to help you make more friends. I did promise you, I would help with that!" she says.

"Great, what do I do?" I ask.

"Start by saying 'hi' to more people," she says.

"Okay, fly away before anyone sees you," I beg, as I see Ryan walking toward the bus stop.

"Don't worry. I'm invisible to everyone else," she laughs.

"What about my math test?" I whisper hurriedly before Ryan reaches.

"Don't worry, if you studied, my magic will work for that too," she says.

In few seconds, Ryan reaches the bus stop and looks up.

"Hi," I say in a low voice.

He smiles and says, "Hey! How's it going?"

I can't believe it!! He finally acknowledged me. My sparrow friend smiles from atop the Stop sign. I widen my eyes at her. I hope Ryan can't see her. Several other kids join at the bus stop and no one seems to notice the sparrow.

At school, I go to my locker to pick up my math binder. Suddenly my sparrow friend is perched above the locker door.

"Are you well prepared for your math test?"

"Stop following me," I laugh.

"Sammy, are you prepared for your math test?"

"Yes, I did work really hard. Are you going to help me remember everything?" I ask pointedly.

"Absolutely am," she responds with a smile.

I rush to my math class. I wave to Becky, who is one of the smartest students in the class. I say a little prayer and wait for the test. I notice a new boy sitting in the front row with shiny, black hair.

The test is much easier than I had imagined. I scored 19 out of 20. I see my sparrow friend perched on the projector screen in the class. *Not too bad.* I signal a thumbs-up to her.

Becky looks at me puzzled wondering why I was giving the projector screen a thumbs-up. I force a smile in embarrassment. She must think I'm crazy.

Then suddenly... poof! My sparrow friend disappears again.

"Huh," I shout. Becky looks at me even more confused.

I smile embarrassed and bury my head in a book but I can't stop smiling about my math score.

On the way home, I see Zach on the bus-stop and want to give him a hug. But he is busy with his friends and does not even look at me.

He races ahead and reaches home. I run inside eagerly with a huge smile and give him an enormous hug. He looks totally confused and I tell him about my score. He smiles at me. I can tell he is proud.

It's the next day and English is my first class for today. I sit in my spot in the back row. Mr. Madison starts teaching us about essays.

I notice the same new boy I saw in math class, sitting in the front row. His shining, black hair reminds me of Charlie.

I wonder what Charlie must be doing in New York. I think I should say 'hi' to the new boy. Could he feel lost...? Just like me on my first day.

After the class, I walk over to the new boy, "Hi, are you new at the school?"

Every Sparrow Was Made to Fly

The shiny haired boy turns around, looks at me and flashes his pearly white teeth.

I freeze. "Whoa! What are you doing here?"

Charlie speaks in a soft, deep voice, "Hi Sammy, how's it going? We just moved here unexpectedly. How are you?"

I think this is the first time he actually spoke to me. I'm really nervous and excited at the same time. *Thank goodness, he knows my name.*

Charlie continues, "My dad is in a two-year research program at Johns Hopkins University so we all decided to move with him. How's life around here? Do you like Virginia so far?"

I stutter a bit nervously. "Life is pretty good. I love Virginia," I lie, looking away from his face.

"Terrific!" he says.

"I am going to my History class now. Bye!" I run off before I blabber some nonsense. I hope he couldn't tell I was blushing.

I felt a shiver of excitement. Charlie is my classmate!!! The Charlie I saw once a year would be in my math and English class for the whole year.

I always thought he was stuck-up, but he spoke rather nicely to me today. I wonder if he would be nice, the next time we meet. Wait! Was he really not a snob all along? I guess... I'll find out!

I sit at my lunch table. Kim comes and joins me. We talk a little and then she starts talking to another girl at the table.

I look dreamily at the floor and my mind wanders. *What am I going to do about the Bollywood classes?* I have to call today. I am also very worried about the weekend and having to learn to bike. What excuse am I going to make so Papa won't insist on biking. I hope it rains... a lot!

I see someone approaching. I look up and it's Charlie.

"Hi!" I say, trying not to stutter.

"How'd you do on your math test yesterday? I got an A+," he says.

*Hmph!!* Suddenly I imagine Charlie as a peacock. Spreading his feathers, he is proudly dancing around the cafeteria. I imagine him singing, "Look at my math score! I'm so cool. I'm the best! Look at my hair, and look at my style."

I start giggling and Charlie looks totally confused. Kim grins too. Charlie gives us a weird look and walks to the next table.

*Sammy did you just mess up your chance at being Charlie's friend?* I think with a sigh.

That evening I hug my coral necklace happily. My sparrow friend, you have helped me find my new friend Kim and you helped me in math. I even said hi to Ryan... and I think you had something to do with Charlie moving here as well.

I still have to figure out the bike and the Bollywood classes, but that's okay. I'm sure you will help me find a way out.

But... there's just one more problem though. Charlie is going to think I am just weird.

*How am I going to make up for my stupidity and get him to talk to me again?*

# 10

# At the Park

All of Zach's tutoring is helping me in math. I have even started liking math... just a little bit though! I discuss math concepts with Becky at recess. Kim is not very enthusiastic about joining our discussion. Most of the ballet dancers give us weird looks, but I don't care. Julia on the other hand looks at us very thoughtfully. *I wonder what's on her mind.*

Becky and I race to see who can solve a Sudoku puzzle first. Ryan joins us at the table and cheers us. Becky wins hands down.

Slowly we have a math group at lunch. I increase my daily practice from twenty minutes to forty minutes at home. It's time for the next math quiz. I get a perfect score.

I am so excited that I even enroll in the Math Tournament with Becky. Ryan asks us at lunch if we have room for him on our team. Becky and I look at each other and nod. Kim asks me to help her with equations. I'm more than happy to help. It looks like I am falling in love... with *math*!

Of course it's Friday today. Which means the weekend is here, and I will need to go biking with Papa. It does not look like it is going to rain in Reston today.

Soon it's time for me to go to the park. I don't see my sparrow friend anywhere. Papa is very excited about taking me to the park. I get ready to leave and wear the uncomfortable helmet.

At the park, I wobble on my bike as Papa holds it in place. A bunch of teenagers whisper to each other and giggle.

"Look at the big girl on the little bike with training wheels," says one teenage boy with a nose ring.

"Isn't she precious?" a girl says with a giggle. She raises her cell phone and snaps a picture of Papa and me. Papa doesn't seem to notice or even be bothered. I feel my cheeks grow hot with embarrassment. I get off the bike and hold on to my ankle.

"I think I have a sprain," I tell Papa, avoiding his eyes.

*I hope he can't tell I'm fibbing.* I really need to go home, away from this horrible park.

I don't know what Papa was thinking when they got me this bike as a gift. *What a horrible gift.* We walk home and drag the bike along with us. I can't tell if Papa is mad.

When I reach home, I limp into my room. Mamma shouts from the kitchen, "Don't forget to call Bolly Mania today."

Oh my! This horrible day hasn't ended yet? Where is my sparrow friend when I need her? Why couldn't she do some magic on those annoying teenagers at the park?

I limp into the hall and sit at the dining table with my math books, so Mamma can see me. She is going to be pleased with me working on math. She loves it so much when I study that soon she will forget all about Bolly Mania.

At first, I work on the problems just to escape calling the dance studio, but after some time I really enjoy the problems. I bury my head in my math book and soon all my problems disappear. I am having fun with equations and variables. I look up and see my sparrow friend on the mantle.

I open my mouth to shout with surprise but cover my mouth so Mamma doesn't hear me.

My sparrow friend sparkles and writes in the air with magic glitter…. "Call Bolly Mania"

# 11

## Robbie Kapoor, here I come!

"H.. h.. Hello!" I whisper, clutching the phone.

"Bollywood Mania, this is Preet... how can I help you?"

"I am calling about Bollywood classes."

"Yes of course, we have continuous enrollments. How old is the child?"

"Child...! I am twelve. Am I too old to start?"

"No, we have classes for all ages and grown-ups too. What is your name?"

"Sammy... Samelda Matthew," I answer. "My mom has already paid for the Thursday class at 6.30

PM. I want to ask about the dress code." He asks for some more information and finds my registration.

"Oh, this class only needs comfortable clothes. No traditional attire is needed," he says.

"Do you need any previous experience?" I ask him.

"Absolutely not, this class has beginners too. We let student progress at different paces. This is a fusion class and has some basic classical steps as well."

"Okay. Thank you," I say. I almost drop the phone as I hang up.

"What am I doing?" I mutter. Fusion! That involves Indian classical and Bollywood. That's even worse than just Bollywood.

I am certain I would look really odd trying the 'jhatkas' and 'matkas', the hip-shaking Bollywood moves. I'm sure the other students were going to laugh at my awkward moves. I should just call them back and cancel.

But of course that did not happen. Soon...Thursday arrives! I dress in my black sweatpants and tie up my unruly hair. Mamma is thrilled and offers to give me a ride. I crackle my knuckles in my room and then finally go down the stairs.

"This is not a good idea," I mutter.

As Mamma drives me over, I look up at the bright green neon sign of the dance studio that read 'Bolly Mania'. I see my sparrow friend waving at me atop the sign.

"I smile. Well I guess I could try one class," I say to myself. I take a deep breath and push the glass door and enter in. I sign my name in the register and walk into the class.

Several students were already practicing. I think I am easily the student, who knows the least.

Why did they have to have mirrors? I wonder! I look prettier in my bedroom mirror. I should have put some lipstick, but Mamma thinks I am too young for that.

The instructor comes in. "Welcome to all of you" she says in a cheerful voice.

"Some words of advice for all newcomers... Don't look at each other. Just go with what your body will allow you to do," she says.

*Easy for you to say, you probably weigh less than hundred pounds even with all that chunky Indian jewelry*, I think to myself.

"We will start with basic Indian classical steps. Watch me and repeat after me."

"Thai ya Thai hi... Thai ya Thai hi."

Several routines continue for half an hour. The instructor continues, "I will correct you if you need to improve any steps. Feel the music and enjoy the dance." We continue to follow the beats.

*Robbie Kapoor, here I come!*

"Most importantly, students, dance like nobody is watching," the instructor continues. Then we have a break.

I peek at myself in the mirror. My cheeks seem a little red with all the exercise. Maybe it's just the music, or the feeling of actually dancing in a crowd. Strangely, I'm feeling a little happy.

As the instructor had said, if I didn't worry about others, I did feel comfortable. It's a good thing I didn't know anyone in the class.

This is beginning to seem like a good idea …until I see a girl sipping some water in the corner. I feel like burying myself in the hardwood floors. It's Julia, the 'popular' Julia from school. Why is she here? Isn't she a ballet dancer?

I turn my face away to look at some posters on the wall. Maybe she won't recognize me. Nobody knows me anyway. The break will end soon, we will go back to our spots and I will take my position at the

103

back of the room and she would not see me. My secret would be safe.

"Hi, Sammy," came a voice from behind. I freeze.

I turn around. Is Julia going to tease me?

"Can you please not tell anyone at school that I'm taking Bollywood Fusion classes?" says Julia.

"Huh?" I say.

"My ballet friends would tease me to death. They don't think Bollywood classifies as a real dance form because we are classical ballet students."

"Oh… " I say, taken aback.

"Yes, they think it's too disorganized and they would ridicule me. But, I love the energy, the free movement, and the songs. Sammy, can you please keep this a secret."

I couldn't believe my ears. "Of course, Julia," I almost laugh with relief. "Your secret is safe with me."

Julia looks relieved. "Thanks!" she says.

I look at her and then say, "But can you also keep this a secret, that I am taking dance classes."

"Of course, Sammy," Julia says in surprise. "But …why?"

"I am certain everyone will laugh at me for trying to dance because I am… well… awkward," I reply.

"Oh! Bollywood is about fun. Being a beginner doesn't matter. You will get better with practice. But your secret is safe with me as well," Julia replies.

"Thanks Julia," I say.

We go back to our spots and the dancing continues. It was a strange feeling. Julia and I were so different from each other, but we both shared the same desire to dance, and both had similar fears. I am shocked that Julia would worry about being teased. Someone as popular as Julia, also has fears?

For the next 30 minutes, we dance to several Bollywood songs that are refreshing and fun. As we dance, I look up and suddenly see my sparrow friend joining us with her Bollywood moves. I laugh and an unsuspecting lady looks at me bewildered.

The instructor says, "Last song for the day." This time it's a peppy, fast song that's so much fun. We are almost breathless after this routine but we all enjoy it thoroughly. The class concludes and the teacher gives pointers for practice at home. I feel happy and refreshed.

As I wait for Mamma to pick me up, I see my sparrow friend waving at me from the dashboard of Mamma's car. I widen my eyes and admonish her with my look. It's a good thing Mamma can't see her or she would freak out.

"How was your class?" Mamma asks.

"It was cool," I reply. My first class has truly been better than I imagined. My fears seem silly now. I also have a new friend, a 'popular' girl. Well, a kind-of friend. I hope Julia will keep her side of the promise.

Nevertheless, I have made a new beginning, a small step in a new direction. Robbie Kapoor, you would be proud of me! Maybe, I was made to dance. I am going to follow my heart. I am going to try to get better at it.

# 12

# A Different Meaning

My sparrow friend does not appear again for a few days, although I try several times to invoke the magic. She did say she would only come when I really needed her. I want to tell Layla about my sparrow friend but I can't. Sometimes, I still wonder if I imagined all of it.

The next day after school, I see Julia in the bus. The seat next to her is empty. I wonder if I should say hi. She looks up and smiles at me. I sit next to her.

"Explain to me again, why you do not want

your friends to know about your Bollywood dance lessons?" I question.

"They would think I am not serious about my classical ballet career," she replies. "You know everyone thinks I am so popular, but deep down inside, I know everyone likes me only because I am pretty. They don't see beyond my perfect features and my ballet dancing."

"I didn't realize you could be unhappy, Julia. You seem like you have everything!" I reply.

Julia continues, "What if I met with an accident and my face looked different? Would my friends still be the same? Would I still be so popular? Would the boys who wait in line to talk to me, still want to be friends with me? All this attention for 'pretty' Julia is not genuine. I am so much more. I yearn to be recognized for who I am from within. But I always have to act a certain way with my friends. I just want to be myself."

I let what she said sink in. "Wow," I think to myself. I didn't realize popular kids have these types of fears too.

In my heart, I feel thankful for having Layla as my BFF. Even if we are a thousand miles apart, we are just a phone call away and I can always be myself.

"Well, I'm sorry you feel this way Julia. I hope something changes and you can be yourself."

"There is one more thing..." Julia says with a pause.

"Okay?" I reply.

"I want to tell them... I like *math*," she says with a big sigh.

I look at her in shock. "Really...?"

"If I ever told them this truth, they would immediately call me a geek and stop hanging out with me," she says gazing at the metal floor of the bus.

"I didn't realize you like math?" I ask in surprise.

"Yes and I would love to compete with you all at Sudoku during recess," she laughs.

I look at her in surprise. Her face quickly changes to a dreamy look as she stares outside the school bus window.

She continues…"I wish, I had a real friend, who didn't care if my hair was set; or if I was wearing makeup; someone who valued me for who I really was. I yearn to just be myself."

The bus reaches my stop. I get off and wave to Julia. Back home, I sip some chocolate milk and look outside, through my kitchen window.

I am surprised that Julia would be so lonely or so troubled. I'd accept her for who she is, but she doesn't know me well enough. I wish she had a sparrow friend too.

Speaking of which, I haven't seen my sparrow friend in a couple of days. *I wonder where she is.*

It's the next day. Becky, Ryan and I start working on our math in the Library. Charlie swings by and asks us if he can join as well. We look at each other and nod. The maximum team size is five so have room for him.

I realize that he is not stuck-up after all. Just a little vain and still very cute! Thankfully, he seems to have forgotten about my silly laughter in the cafeteria as well.

Becky and Ryan have to leave to get ready for gym class. Charlie and I are alone studying geometry. We study about lines and rays.

Charlie mumbles, "Two parallel lines never meet. When two lines meet at 90 degrees they are perpendicular."

"What did you just say, Charlie?"

"Huh, these are fifth grade basics. I am just reviewing them mentally. What's up Sammy?"

I have an Archimedes moment. I almost want to shout Eureka… "When two lines meet at 90 degrees they are perpendicular," I say excitedly, almost yelling.

"Shush… We are in the library. Do you want us to get kicked out?" Charlie says with an exasperated sigh. I laugh joyfully. Charlie looks at me confused.

"What's up with the laughter?" he asks.

"You've given me a clue to solve a mystery that has been haunting me. I will explain later. Sorry!"

I run to my next class and wait impatiently for the school day to be over. I ride the bus home and rush home eagerly and run upstairs to my painting.

*'When they meet',* Great Grand-Uncle Johnson may have been a math geek like Zach and me. *He was talking about the coconut trees.* I take two rulers and extend each coconut tree and they meet at a spot on the top section of the metallic frame. I feel my hands on the spot on the inner side of the frame, and there was a slight dent there. I stick my fingernail through it

and the heavy metallic frame shifts with a faint creak. My heart races. I expect some sort of diamond to show up.

All our problems with losing the mansion will be over. Maybe it will be shiny, like the Kohinoor diamond, the most precious diamond from India that is in the British queen's crown today.

I feel the bottom of the opening and an old ruffled up paper is stuck there. I fear it might almost fall apart. I open it gently and it says, *'When they meet again at 4'.*

What! Is this some kind of joke. Was Great Grand-Uncle Johnson a comedian or a math geek?

The next day at school, I tell Kim and my math team about the mansion, my painting and this new mystery. This new message definitely needs more brains to think. Of course, I can't tell them about my sparrow friend. They are all at loss on what this new message means.

# 13

# Julia's Surprise

I put the message carefully in an envelope and store it in my bookshelf along with the painting. I don't want to spend any more time on a goose chase, at least for a few days.

Today is Thursday again, and I have dance class. It's been a few weeks of class and I now I have begun to feel excited about the class. I see my sparrow friend greet me again on the Bolly Mania sign, as Mamma drives me over. I wave slightly to her. I should ask her about the mystery message when we talk again. She might be able to help. I get ready for class and I'm bold enough to take a position in the front row. Julia takes a position next to me. We talk as we dance.

"Sammy, would you guys be willing to try me out for your Math Tournament team? You can give me a trial test," she says biting her lip.

I look at her in surprise. "Would you really like to join? Are you ready to work on it?"

She nods, "Yes, I want to."

"You don't need a test as long as you are ready to work on it.  If you are weak then you can practice," I say.

"Yes, I really like math. I may need a little practice but I will work hard," she says.

"The most important thing is how much effort you are ready to put into it," I say.

"It's what I want to do," she says. "My dad is a mathematician, but I don't get to see him much, ever since my parents separated. I really enjoy math though.

It's what I dream of doing when I am older. Thanks for your trust."

"What about your friends?" I ask.

"Yes, that is still a problem," she replies. "They still don't know about my Bollywood classes either."

"Oh," I reply.

"You know... let's forget it. It won't work out," she says in a disappointed voice.

"Julia, once a friend told me, you have to believe good things will happen to you and it will. You have to be ready to take risks in order to gain something."

Julia looks thoughtful.

"Don't hold yourself back. You were made to do what your heart desires!" I say.

I look up at the top of the mirror and my sparrow friend applauds me. I can tell she is proud of me. I remember her words... *Be a good friend to others and you will make plenty of friends.*

119

Our class ends and we all go home. I hope Julia's friends can accept her for who she is. I am happy I could reassure her.

A week later in recess, there is another surprise waiting for us... the good kind!

Alicia, Julia's friend asks me, "Hey Sammy, you moved recently from India right?"

"Why," I raise my eyebrow and say.

"Do you know Bolly-something dance?" she continues.

"You mean Bollywood?" I ask.

"Yes, do you know Bollywood dance?"

*Why are they asking?*

"Maybe..." I say. "Why?"

"We watched some reruns of Miss America yesterday. An American-Indian contestant won it a couple of years ago and danced to a Bollywood song," Megan says.

"I can't remember the name of the song," Alicia continues, "we thought it was pretty cool. Different from what we have always seen at Miss America contests."

"It was Dhoom Tana," I say.

"Yes... that was it. We watched in awe," Megan says. "We are thinking of adding that to the pantomime. Do you think you could teach us some Bollywood moves?"

Sheba and Joanne overhear Megan. "We would like to learn some Bollywood too."

I look in shock at them. Julia is right behind me and hears them too. "So you all want to learn Bollywood?" she asks the group of girls.

"Yes!" Megan says.

Julia looks at me and takes a deep breath. I signal her reassuringly with my eyes. She nods.

"Yes, we can both teach you Bollywood dance," Julia says.

121

"Wait...what! Julia, you know Bollywood dance?" Alicia says. Megan widens her eyes.

Julia speaks up, "Yes, I didn't think you both would ever think that it was a good thing. I have been taking lessons, but I am still very serious about my classical ballet career."

"Oh come on, why didn't you tell us?" Alicia says.

"I thought you guys would be disappointed in me and think I don't care about ballet anymore... or not want to be friends with me," Julia says.

Megan sounds alarmed, "Do you think we are like the mean girls in the movies?"

Julia and I laugh.

"So you both can teach us Bollywood?" Megan says.

"Huh! Julia dances Bollywood?" one of the ballet dancers from eighth grade sneers. We hadn't noticed her standing there. Julia's shoulder freezes and she wishes to disappear into the ground.

Alicia comes to her rescue. "Yes, she is multitalented and can do ballet and Bollywood dance."

Megan pitches in "Can *you* do both?"

The eighth grader shrugs and walks off. All of us giggle.

"Julia, do you think we could talk to the resource teacher and start an after school dance program," I say. "That way we could all practice after class."

"That sounds great, Sammy!"

She looks at her friends, "Alicia, Megan, I'm sorry I didn't trust you with this," Julia says.

"Don't worry about it," Alicia says.

"But, we have another question," Megan says. "We see you look dreamily at the geeky math table? Do you have a crush on one of those boys?"

"Huh," Julia says, "of course not!"

"Then what's the deal with that look?" Alicia asks.

"Tell them Julia," I whisper.

Julia takes a deep breath... "It's not a crush. It's love... I love *math*," Julia says softly.

"Oh!!!" they both say.

"Are you guys disappointed in me?" Julia asks.

"Why would we be disappointed? And why didn't you say anything before?" Megan says.

"I thought you both wouldn't want to be friends with me anymore... if I was a math geek."

"Julia! We've known each other since kindergarten. Why would that matter?"

"Well we don't have any friends who are math geeks. All our friends are mostly from our dance troupe."

"Yeah... but that's only because we always hang out with them," Alicia says.

"I guess... I judged you too quickly," Julia says sadly. "I'm sorry... so you guys are cool with me being on a math team?"

"As long as you are on time for your dance rehearsals," Megan says with a laugh.

I smile happily at how all of this turned out. Sometimes our fears are just our mind playing tricks on us. I'm happy I was able to help Julia, in a small way and she could finally be herself with her friends.

And Bollywood dance will soon become a part of my reality with the after-school club. After all dancing with Robbie Kapoor has been my dream since I was nine. I see my sparrow friend wink at me atop the locker. I smile. *Giving simple advice and encouragement, I guess that's what being a true friend means.* Thank-you my sparrow friend! Thanks for helping me and helping me help Julia ...

# 14

# Who is old now?

Julia has joined our math team. We are preparing for the Math Tournament. Becky and Ryan have become good friends. I notice that Julia has a special liking for Ryan. Of course, it's best for us to all just stay as good friends at this age. There were several more years ahead for crushes and love. Once I realized this, I stopped being silly around Charlie and we have become good friends too. Of course, Layla does not believe me when I say that, and continues to tease me.

Our team wins the tournament and qualifies for the Regional Tournament. Becky is a super whiz and we all pitch in as well. I think my sparrow friend is definitely helping me with answers. As I study on my desk in the afternoon, she startles me with a sudden appearance.

"Hello Sammy!" she says.

"Hello, my dear friend," I reply with a smile.

"What do you need today, Sammy?"

I take a deep breath. "You've helped me in math and to make friends. I am really grateful. But, I think I need to study on my own now... with no magic. We are competing at tournaments and I think it would be unfair for me to have your magic spell on me."

"Are you sure you can do this on your own?" the sparrow asks.

"Yes," I nod confidently.

"Okay," she says and mumbles some words and a blue light falls on me, with a whoosh.

"Am I supposed to feel weak?" I ask my sparrow friend. "Have I lost my math powers?"

"No, you will feel stronger, because now you will have the powers from within. You won't depend on me, but on yourself. Take a deep breath and you will feel stronger. Honesty will give you the power to accomplish anything."

*Honesty will give you the power to accomplish anything,* I think to myself. I'll have to figure out what she means later.

"Okay, there's one more thing... there's a new mystery message I found in the painting. I put it away because I couldn't figure it out and I'm so disappointed. Do you know about it and can you help me figure it out?" I ask.

"Sammy, yes I do know about it. You have already taken the first step to be on your own feet by asking me to take away your math powers. You have the power within you to solve this mystery. All I can tell you is... a treasure awaits you my precious girl! I won't appear again but I will always be watching over you!"

"You won't appear again? Why?" I ask.

"Yes, my job is done here Sammy. You have found your own wings. Now you can achieve anything you want because you have the confidence from within," she says and flies over to my side. She nuzzles her head against my cheek. "Goodbye Sammy!"

"I will miss you my dear friend." I reply and gently stroke her head.

"I will always be with you. You just won't see me. Just remember… don't worry about stuff. Be positive. Each one of us was made to follow our dreams. Every single one of us was made to do great things!"

"I will try to remember that always," I say.

"Great!" she says.

And poof! She disappears again.

My sparrow friend was right. I didn't feel weak, I felt stronger about math. I had made friends. I am dancing okay. Even popular kids have started talking to me. Yes, I did feel stronger. Like, I could survive in America. I take a deep breath. I sleep peacefully that night.

I keep thinking about my sparrow friend's words that week. On the weekend, we have a multi-cultural potluck party, organized by Papa's office.

All the employees can bring any food of their choice from any country. I am really thrilled about this event. Mamma makes her mouthwatering Butter Chicken and scrumptious Paneer Curry. We can even dress in traditional outfits for the party.

We arrive at the party and sample foods from different parts of the world. I taste delicious Vietnamese Sesame Cold Noodles, Mediterranean Gyros, Mexican Enchiladas, Italian Cannoli and American Pot Pie.

I had never tasted so many international dishes or cuisines in my life. Potlucks are common in America but are not common in India. I realize that while neighbors don't go to each other's homes with food plates in America, a potluck is a great idea for sharing food.

I gradually realize that America is a mixture of cultures, and there is an opportunity for me to learn about different cultures of the world here. Every culture and country has its own advantages.

I accompany Mamma to the grocery store on some days. I begin to understand why Mamma likes America. It is easier to buy good quality groceries with one trip to the supermarket. The amenities are great.

Dishes at home are also getting easier as I learn to use the dishwasher properly. We also have cleaning services now, to clean the house every 2 weeks. While we do not have the help of a maid all the time, I start feeling a sense of accomplishment when I clean my closet or my messy table.

Slowly, I begin to appreciate America. I am thankful for the clean sidewalks, the polite customer service at stores, and the orderly traffic patterns.

Now, I understand now why my parents were excited about moving here. I realize why Layla was happy for me! Why our neighbors and friends were thrilled about us coming here and why so many of them came to send us off at the airport.

Yes it was because they loved us, but also because they were happy about us moving to the 'Land of Dreams'.

I still miss Goa terribly, but I begin to love my new country too and appreciate the great things about it. My heart had always been in Goa, but now I feel I had actually landed in America.

There was just one huge problem. I still couldn't ride a bike. But as my sparrow friend said, I can try to find solutions to my problems.

And then I look at my painting. Yes… there's still another huge problem. My favorite mansion is still up for sale in two months. I try invoking the magic of the amulet again to talk to sparrow.

"Sparrow… my friend how can I save Georgy Uncle's mansion?" I ask in despair. But she doesn't appear. Maybe she is relying on me to find the answer myself.

I finish my homework and then switch on the TV. Papa returns back early from work. I greet him happily.

He says, "Sammy let's go biking. It's great weather outside today." My cheerful mood quickly changes to despair and my shoulders droop.

"Papa, I don't want to bike this year. Maybe I can try next summer." Secretly I know I won't do it next summer either. I look out the kitchen window and see other kids zoom by on bikes. I see parents bike with kids as well. *Why do bikes have to be so popular in America?*

Papa holds my chin and looks me in the eye. "What's going on, Sammy?"

Tears flow down my cheek. I try to wipe my eyes but the tears keep coming anyway. I look at Papa. His face is filled with concern. I remember my sparrow friend's words; *Honesty will give you the power to accomplish anything.* I find enough courage to tell Papa the truth.

"Papa, the real reason is I'm too old for training wheels. You always think of me as your baby, but kids in America learn to bike when they are six and seven years old or even younger. I'm too embarrassed to ride that bike. I don't want anyone to mock me. I'm sorry!"

Papa says, "Oh, Sammy, do you know I don't know to bike either? I have been trying to help you

135

balance and learn to bike, but I don't ride one myself. Do you think I'm not a good Papa or do you love me any less? Are you embarrassed about me?"

"Of course not, you are a great Papa. I would never be embarrassed that you didn't know biking. You know so many other things."

"Then don't worry so much," Papa says.

"Just enjoy life as it comes. We will go in two hours okay. I am just going out for an errand."

"Okay, I will be ready when you are back," I reply.

Couple of hours later, I hear Papa's car and I go to the garage. I am going to be brave and try to ignore the teenagers who mock me. I need to take risks if I want to learn something. Papa gets out of his car. He has a surprise for me...

He was standing with a brand-new bike for himself... and it had training wheels!

"Oh, Papa, are you serious?"

136

"Well, you are never too old for anything!" he exclaims. I giggle happily.

Together we start trying to learn to balance at the park. I watch as Papa falls right into a grassy green bush at the end of the path. My eyes widen in horror, but Papa just gets up laughing.

The teenagers look at Papa and then seem to be busy with some other conversation. Papa keeps trying to balance and I feel bold enough to try myself. I work hard on my balancing skills.

The next day we both come to the park again. I imagine myself riding the bike before I actually do it. We both have trouble, but a lot of fun too. Soon I learn to totally ignore the teenagers.

I enjoy the breeze blowing my short, dark hair and the gentle sunlight kissing my cheeks. It feels good to be on the playground with my bike.

We watch some online videos on biking. One shows us how to go down a slope and not pedal, just practice balancing. That video helps us both.

I meet my math team every day after school, and then I go with Papa in the evenings. I keep the 'learning to ride a bike', a secret from my friends. I know my sparrow friend would want me to be brave and share that, but I am not ready for that yet.

After a few weeks I can take off one of my training wheels. Another three weeks later, my other training wheel comes off. I fall a couple of times into the same bush that Papa fell into, but I laugh just like Papa did. It isn't embarrassing anymore. I take a deep breath and keep working on my balancing skills. Finally, I learn to bike.

"Yes, you are never too old for training wheels," I say aloud to myself. I am now the happiest biker in Little Park.

I am beginning to feel like a bird that learned to fly again. I have conquered my little dreams of learning to dance, learning to ride a bike, making new friends...

And yes, Papa is the second happiest biker in Little Park!

# 15

# An Unusual Video Call

Our tournament day is soon approaching. We have a meeting and math practice in my basement. My friends had heard all about the mystery message I had found in the painting, but none of them had actually seen it.

Becky asks, "Sammy, can you show us your ancient mystery painting?" I bring the painting carefully downstairs, along with the faded paper from the painting and show it to my friends. This is the first time Julia was hearing about the mystery, so I quickly fill her in on the details. She is mesmerized by the painting as well.

"When they meet again at 4," she reads the writing aloud.

"I'm sorry I have no clue what it means," Ryan says looking at me.

"So the first meeting was the two lion paws and that gave you an amulet?" asks Charlie

"And the second meeting was the two trees and that gave you this note," says Becky.

"Well there was another one too but I am not allowed to talk about it," I say uncomfortably. *My sparrow friend had warned me that I couldn't tell anyone about her.*

"So now we are talking about a fourth meeting?" Ryan asks. "Is that what the 4 means?"

"Why would it say 'at 4'?" Julia questions.

"Forget it guys, I don't think I can save the mansion," I say disappointedly.

That night, I wish for my sparrow friend to appear, but she doesn't show up. *I miss her but all her advice is still with me.*

I look at the paper again. What does this mean, 'When they meet again at 4'?

Just then, Layla sends me a text. Her family is going over to Georgy Uncle's mansion to help him pack. The resort owners are coming for a final walk-through of the mansion. All the paperwork has been prepared. I feel a knot in my stomach. Tears start filling inside my eyes, but I hold them back.

"Can you video chat me when you get there?" I ask. "It's past midnight here in America, but its mid-morning in India right?"

"Okay," she messages back. "I will, in a few hours."

I toss and turn in my bed waiting for her call. The memories of the mansion flash before my eyes. I remember collecting shells on the shore. I can hear the sound of the waves in my ears. I remember racing away from the waves, and then the waves catching up to me. Childhood laughter echoes in my room.

I hold my amulet and wait for my sparrow friend to arrive. She does not come. But I remember her words... *You can face the challenges and solve your problems. Every one of us was made to do great things.*

Let me check if Zach is still awake. He may have ideas. I open my bedroom door and see the light is still on in his room. His door was slightly ajar. He is playing a video game.

"Zach, the mansion has a walk-through today. They will sign the papers soon," I signal to him.

"Huh!" he looks in confusion. He has no idea what I am trying to say. He puts down his headphones and looks at me with a puzzled expression.

"Zach, the mansion has a walk-through today. They will sign the papers soon," I say aloud.

"Oh!" he says and puts his head down.

"Come to my room," I say.

"Ok!" he says and follows me to my room. I show him the painting and the new message.

"Why didn't you show this to me before?" he asks.

"Well, you were never interested in my mystery from the beginning," I respond.

I message my friends, "Crisis! My favorite mansion in India is to be sold soon. Contract will be signed shortly. Last few hours to decode the mystery message. Come immediately. Need your brain power ASAP."

Zach shakes his head in disbelief. "Are you going to call everyone home at this hour? It's too late in the night. You've had weeks to solve the mystery message. How is anything going to change tonight?"

"Zach, never give up hope. You must take risks if you want to gain something."

"We will be there," several of them respond. Zach and I tiptoe downstairs and go to the basement with the painting.

Within 30 minutes, I hear some scratching noises at our backyard gate. I open the basement patio door to let my friends in.

Charlie, Julia, Ryan, Kim and Becky are all here. Every one showed up. Zach closes the door that leads up to the main level from the basement, so our parents don't hear us, but we are afraid to turn the lights on. Our cell phone lights guide each other.

"This is so exciting," Becky says.

"It feels like a movie," Kim adds.

"Now all we need is some crazy zombies at the window outside," Charlie whispers.

"Stop," Julia laughs.

"You kids are crazy," Zach admonishes us. "Sammy what do you expect will happen in the last minute. We've had six months to save the mansion and you guys have had weeks to decode this message."

"Zach, someone one day told me we can solve any challenge, if we believe we can. Maybe this challenge was meant to be solved in the last minute. We can do this together."

Ta Ta Taa Ta Ta, my cell phone rings. Everyone gets startled with the ring. "Sorry I changed the ring tone to an upbeat drum beat this morning."

"Shush, reduce the volume," Zach scolds. "You are so going to get us all grounded."

It was Layla on video chat. I introduce my BFF to all my friends. She tells us it is 3 PM in India. She is at the beach in the afternoon sun. "Oh I can hear the seagulls caw," I sigh.

I have the faded paper with me. I am also wearing my amulet. I hold it and say a little prayer. "Great Grand-uncle what did you mean?" I exclaim.

We put the paper on a table and circle around it, trying to think of meanings.

147

In my mind I say, "My sparrow friend, where are you? You said you had the magic of the seas. Show me how to save the mansion."

Suddenly there is a commotion on Layla's end. A few men and women in business suits are walking on the mansion porch.

"It's Mr. Evelmore. The rich industrialist from Delhi," Layla whispers. "He has built many five-star resorts in Goa already. I am going to put you guys on mute, so they don't hear you."

"What are those boxes?" a lady from the group asks.

"Those are all the pirate artifacts," Georgy Uncle says. "I packed them up because you said the little museum area would be converted to a spa."

"Oh! That's a bunch of trash fit for a flea market," Mr. Evelmore says.

Georgy Uncle looks tense and bites his lip. He does not reply. Zach and I look at each other sadly.

Layla walks back to the beach through the double gated entrance with the lion sculptures.

I close my eyes. My sparrow does not appear, but I remember our conversations...

*You have found your wings. You can solve all your challenges.*

I scratch my head thinking of the other things she has told me... *You can find all the solutions to your problems, if you believe you can.*

Aww man! *How? What did she mean?*

"Okay, let us step through this one by one," Ryan says, and breaks me out of my reverie. Charlie looks at the paper and reads aloud, "When they meet again at 4."

"So the lions met first, then something else met and then the coconut trees met on the frame right?" asks Julia.

"Yes," I respond softly.

Layla speaks up, "Can you guys show me the coconut trees on the painting." Kim picks up the phone to show the painting to Layla.

"What are those sculptures in the behind Layla?" Kim asks me.

I look at her and shrug. "Oh, those are the lion sculptures on the gate. The lions on the painting frame are a replica of those lions."

"It looks like the lions are teasing us," Charlie says.

"I've always been afraid of those lions and their shadows," I say with a laugh.

"When they meet again at 4," Becky says.

We hear the big, ancient clock at the nearby church chime through Layla's phone. The clock strikes. I count one, two, three and four.

And then I freeze.

"When they meet again at 4," I whisper to myself.

The lion paws met first to give me the amulet. The shadows meet at different times in the afternoon but exactly at 4 PM, there would be a spot on the ground that both the paws meet.

"Layla turn around! Check if the paws meet at a spot on the ground... right at this time!" I say with a shriek.

We all see the spot on the sandy ground that the shadows of the paws meet at.

"Layla, go... go... get a shovel," Zach says. Layla runs into the outhouse storage area and returns with a couple of shovels.

We yell excitedly. "Dig, Dig!" She looks at us and says, "Relax guys, I am trying my best. I've never even used these shovels before."

She keeps digging and digging. Becky starts to bite her nails. After 10 minutes, Layla hits a clank.

She retrieves a box and opens it quickly. "Oh, there's another paper."

151

"Darn! Don't tell me this is another clue," I shout.

"Shush," Zach says. "Don't wake up the house."

"It's some sort of map, and it is all faded. It's also pretty huge and folded many times over," Layla says.

I didn't even want to read it.

"Let me just check if it's a treasure map," Layla says.

"Huh!" there's no treasure, Layla" I reply gloomily.

"Yes, it looks like a regular map with countries. There is no treasure symbol or anything to indicate it is a treasure map," she says disappointedly.

"Toss it back in the box," I tell Layla.

"Gosh! What a disappointment!" Julia says.

"I'm done reading messages," Becky says.

Zach looks gloomy, "Great Grand-Uncle Johnson must have had a weird sense of humor."

"At least let's give the box to Georgy Uncle. It looks nice," Layla says. "Shall I end the call, guys?"

Just then Georgy Uncle comes to the patio. Mr. Evelmore and his team have just left the mansion.

"Is that Sammy? Hello children, why are you awake at this hour?"

"It's a long story, Georgy Uncle," I say sadly.

"We thought we found a treasure, but it's really an old paper that looks like a map," Layla says. She tells him the story quickly.

Georgy Uncle replies thoughtfully, "Layla, can you check if there is any writing on the map?" Layla lays the map on the patio table and opens it out eight times.

"Guys, I still have you on the call because I am checking the map again," she tells us. She peers across the writing. We all crowd around the phone and try to catch a glimpse of the map.

"All the writing seems to be in Portuguese," Layla exclaims. She moves the phone over the map so I can read it too. I look in one corner and say out aloud, "V. Da Gama."

"What?" Georgy Uncle says.

"V. Da Gama, that's what it says right there," I say.

"This is no ordinary map, Sammy. This is the map used by Vasco Da Gama, when he first discovered Goa," he shouts with excitement. "This is as precious as it can get."

"Huh," we all say.

"Yes, the map has great significance because it is hand-signed by him and has lot of notes written by him on the sides. It established the first sea-route from Europe to India," Georgy Uncle replies, his eyes sparkling.

"What does it mean for us?" I ask in shock.

"I am sure the Goa Museum of History would pay a fortune for it. We would get at least 10 million Indian rupees. That would be more than enough to keep the mansion," he says with joyful tears in his eyes.

We all look at each other in disbelief! I cannot believe this actually happened.

This was a fun night. I am so thankful to all my friends for their help in solving this mystery. Finally!

Thank-you my sparrow friend, for all the encouragement. I guess miracles do happen if you believe in them. Zach and I hug each other.

# 16

# A Mystical Revelation

It is winter break and we are visiting Goa. Georgy Uncle is hosting Christmas this year. He has made a fortune from the map. He renovated the mansion and also saved up for future years. He is having a huge Christmas party. He even sent us airline tickets to visit him.

Layla is at the airport with her family, and all our friends and relatives to greet us. They welcome us with garlands and sweets. I run over and give Layla a warm hug. I notice Zach blush a little when he sees Layla. I'm wondering ... does he like Layla? Is she his secret crush? Definitely a new mystery for me to solve, I grin.

We first stop by at Layla's home for some tea. Her mom has made Gulab Jamuns, Samosas and lots of goodies for us.

Layla and I watch the beautiful waters of the Indian Ocean from her rooftop. I am happy to be back with my BFF.

I am also excited about celebrating Christmas at the mansion. Georgy Uncle has invited Layla's family as well to live at the mansion. With the new renovations he can host a lot of people. All of us drive over later in the evening. We reach Bambolim, and I run to give Georgy Uncle the biggest hug ever.

The sumptuous dinner set at the table makes us hungry, even though we've already eaten so much at Layla's home. I look at the Chicken 65, Lamb Biriyani and the Vindaloo and my appetite is back.

We relish all the yummy food and indulge in the dessert of Caramel custard. I am happy to be back in Bambolim. But I also feel happy about going back to Virginia after the vacation. We relax on the huge couch. Georgy Uncle calls Papa and me to the patio to show us a surprise gift he bought for me.

I look at my gift in awe… a sleek, silver Fat Tire Beach Cruiser bike, and it had no training wheels.

"Sammy, do you know how much fun it is to learn to bike on beach sand?" he asks eagerly. I smile and look at Papa.

"Georgy Uncle, I do not… but I sure am super excited to find out," I respond.

The evening of eating, singing and laughter concludes. We all go to our rooms and I drift off to sleep.

"Sammy! Sammy!" I hear someone calling out and again I have slipped from the edge of a cliff. I look around… I am still falling in slow motion. The mute button is still on. The scene looks familiar. But this time, I am wearing my coral amulet.

And then, I see a tall mountain in a distance that looks surreal. There are white clouds around it, not gray. I kick my legs and arms... and suddenly my fall slows down. I wave my arms and hold the amulet and close my eyes and suddenly... I have wings. I have turned into a... Sparrow... I wave my arms and soar into the sky.

My wings keep growing and I feel strong. I see meanings of my name written in the sky, floating in the clouds. *Energetic, charismatic, focused, ambitious...* I soar toward the tall mountain. The gentle sunlight embraces me. I continue to fly... and then land gracefully in a green pasture. I have landed on the peak of the tallest mountain... I feel strong. I have conquered my fears. Instead of falling in the valley, I have learned to fly!

# Afterword

When Sammy kept falling from a cliff, she had labelled herself; too big to learn to bike; too awkward to dance; too different with her accent and culture. Then a magical sparrow helps her conquer her fears, make friends, and love her new country.

Later, Sammy asks the sparrow to take her powers away, when she finds inner strength to be successful and fly on her own...In the last chapter, Sammy herself turns into a sparrow. Instead of falling down the cliff, she soars gracefully into the sky and lands on a beautiful pasture.

Who was the magical sparrow? Was it Sammy's soul or conscience? Was it her inner voice? Who are the sparrows in our life, who help us win those battles; help us with multicultural acceptance; encourage us to be successful? Are they our friends and our family? Our inner voices...?

I hope Sammy's story helps you listen to those encouraging voices and go after your dreams. Because... You were Made for Success just like... Every Sparrow Was Made to Fly.

*~ Lin Thomas*

# Glossary for Young readers

Bewildered – Confused or puzzled

Charismatic – Charming and fascinating

Dreary – Dull and boring

Encasing – Enclose or cover in a case

Encompassing – To be on all sides of

Exquisite – Delicate and elegant

Inherited – Received

Inscription – Writing or message

Mesmerized – Charmed or captivated

Mystical – Magical or fascinating

Revelation – A surprise in a dramatic way

Reverie – Daydream

Ruckus – Disturbance

Scrumptious – Tasty and delicious

Stutter- Stammer

Whimsical – Playful or amusing

# Other Publications from Yay Learner LLC

Inspirational Short Stories for Children by Children

## ZEAL

Volume - 1

*Words of wisdom, inspiration and humor from authors that connect to their readers*

NOW AVAILABLE ON AMAZON.COM

# About the Illustrator

Chitra Bhandare is a talented artist and instructor based in Virginia. She is the Founder and owner of Ashburn Art Classes; a Virginia based Art School for kids.

Chitra had a passion for art from a very young age. She graduated from Goa College of Art as a Graphic Designer. She worked as a Lead Animator for a Multinational Company.

She specializes in various mediums including Pastels, Oil Paints, Canvas Paintings and Sketching. Her desire to work with kids and her love for art were the driving forces behind the creation of her Art School. Chitra lives in Virginia with her husband and son.

# Coming Soon

## Yay Learner Presents

## ZEAL

Inspirational Stories for Children by
Children

Volume - 2

# About the Author

Lin Rajan Thomas lived across the street from a library and visited every day after school. That love for books soon transformed into a passion for writing in her school, college, and in her federal consulting career in Washington DC.

Lin is a published author with Chicken Soup for the Pre-Teen Soul 2 of the NY Times best-selling series, published in over 32 languages and 100 countries. She treasures the first fan mail she received from children across the world. She has been the Editor for magazines run by non-profits in the DC area and is also a published author with ProjectManagement.com run by PMI. Lin has a Diploma in Writing for Children from the Institute of Children's Writers.

Lin lives in beautiful Virginia with her husband and 3 children. She truly hopes 'Every Sparrow Was Made to Fly' makes a difference in the lives of all the children she knows. She believes the true meaning of being successful is being happy...